THE LOST DISCIPLE

Judas Iscariot Story

D. DECKKER

Dinsu Books

Copyright © 2024 D. DECKKKER

All rights reserved

This book is a work of historical fiction. While inspired by historical events and figures, it reimagines and dramatizes the life of Judas Iscariot for creative and narrative purposes. Any liberties taken with historical, cultural, or religious contexts are intended to explore universal themes of humanity, faith, and moral conflict. The story should not be interpreted as a theological or historical account.

No part of this book may be reproduced, or stored in a retrieval system, or transmitted in any form or by any means, electronic, mechanical, photocopying, recording, or otherwise, without express written permission of the publisher.

ISBN-13: 9798305743319

Cover design by: D. DECKKER
Printed in the United States of America

For my beloved wife, Subhashini, whose unwavering support and love light my darkest paths, and for my daughter, Sasha, who inspires me to dream bigger and love deeper. This is for both of you—my heart, my hope, my everything.

CONTENTS

Title Page
Copyright
Dedication
Preface

Chapter 1: A World in Chains	1
Chapter 2: The Marketplace Encounter	5
Chapter 3: A Friend Lost	9
Chapter 4: The Spark of Rebellion	13
Chapter 5: The Quiet Voice	17
Chapter 6: The Meeting	21
Chapter 7: Joining the Disciples	25
Chapter 8: Miracles and Questions	29
Chapter 9: Signs of Division	33
Chapter 10: The Kingdom's Cost	37
Chapter 11: Whispers of Betrayal	41
Chapter 12: The Betrayal	44
Chapter 13: The Last Supper	47
Chapter 14: The Garden Confrontation	50
Chapter 15: The Fateful Kiss	53
Chapter 16: Condemned by History	57

Chapter 17: Haunted by Ghosts	60
Chapter 18: The Journey for Redemption	63
Chapter 19: A Vision of Truth	66
Chapter 20: The Final Decision	69
Afterword	73
Acknowledgement	75
About The Author	77
Books By This Author	79

PREFACE

The name Judas Iscariot evokes strong emotions—betrayal, guilt, and condemnation. Yet, behind the infamous kiss lies a human story often overshadowed by his role in history. *The Lost Disciple* seeks to peel back the layers of myth and judgment, exploring the man behind the name.

Set against the turbulent backdrop of 1st-century Judea, this novel reimagines Judas as a deeply conflicted figure, grappling with faith, loyalty, and the weight of choices he cannot undo. His path is not just one of betrayal but also of humanity—marked by doubt, hope, and the desperate search for redemption.

In writing this story, I aim not to excuse Judas's actions but to understand them, to see him as more than a villain. Through his eyes, we examine themes of forgiveness, destiny, and the cost of devotion. This is not just his story—it is a mirror for all of us who have wrestled with our imperfections, seeking light in the darkest moments.

Let us journey together into the life of *The Lost Disciple*. May it challenge, provoke, and ultimately, remind us of the complexity of the human heart.

CHAPTER 1: A WORLD IN CHAINS

The sun hung low over the hills of Kerioth, casting long shadows across the village. Dust swirled through the narrow streets as Judas Iscariot adjusted the straps of the wooden yoke across his shoulders. The baskets balanced at each end were heavy with grain, his family's meager yield after weeks of backbreaking labor. He trudged toward the market square, the weight familiar yet unyielding.

The marketplace buzzed with subdued activity. Merchants hawked their wares in voices that barely rose above the oppressive heat, their eyes darting nervously toward the Roman garrison stationed at the edge of the square. Soldiers leaned against stone walls, their polished armor gleaming under the sun's glare, a silent reminder of the power that loomed over them all.

Judas paused as a commotion erupted near the center of the square. Two soldiers dragged a man forward, his tunic torn and streaked with dirt. A Roman centurion followed, his whip coiled in one hand. The man stumbled, his face contorted in fear, as a soldier shoved him to his knees.

"This one failed to pay his taxes," the centurion declared, his voice cold and detached. "Let this be a lesson to all who think to defy Rome."

The crowd shifted uneasily but remained silent. Judas clenched his fists, the yoke on his shoulders forgotten as anger surged through him. The man's wife stood nearby, clutching a child to her chest, her sobs muffled against the oppressive silence.

"They take everything," Judas muttered under his breath. "And still it's not enough."

"Careful," a voice whispered behind him. Turning, Judas saw a fellow villager, older and hunched with age. "Words like that can get you killed."

Judas's jaw tightened. "And silence will leave us slaves forever."

The centurion raised his whip, and the first lash cut through the air. The man cried out, the sound tearing through the stillness. Judas stepped forward instinctively, but a hand gripped his arm.

"Don't," the villager warned. "There's nothing you can do."

Judas wrenched his arm free but stopped himself. The soldiers would kill him without hesitation. And then what? His father's face flashed in his mind, weary and worn, warning him to think before acting. Reluctantly, he turned away, his chest heaving with unspent rage.

That evening, Judas sat at the wooden table in his family's small home. The aroma of lentil stew filled the air, but he barely touched his food. His father, Simon, sat across from him, his weathered face etched with lines of worry. Beside him, Judas's mother silently ladled stew into their bowls, her movements methodical, her gaze distant.

"They flogged Joseph in the square today," Judas said, breaking the heavy silence.

Simon looked up, his brow furrowing. "Joseph?"

"He couldn't pay his taxes," Judas said bitterly. "They whipped him until he bled, while his wife and child watched. Is this what we've come to?"

Simon sighed, setting his spoon down. "It's the way of things, Judas. Rome is too powerful. There's no use in fighting them."

Judas slammed his hand on the table, the sound startling his mother. "You call this living, Father? Bowing our heads while they grind us into dust? How long are we supposed to endure this?"

"Lower your voice," Simon warned, his tone sharp. "Walls have ears."

"Let them hear!" Judas stood, his chair scraping against the floor. "What do we have left to lose? They take our grain, our money, our dignity. And we're just supposed to accept it?"

"And what would you do?" Simon shot back, his voice rising. "Take up a sword and march against them? You think that will bring freedom? It will bring death. For you, for me, for your mother. Is that the future you want?"

Judas's fists clenched at his sides. "Better to die fighting than to live like this."

"You're a fool if you believe that," Simon said, his voice heavy with frustration. "Freedom doesn't come from reckless defiance. It comes from survival, from endurance. We do what we must to live."

"Living isn't enough," Judas said quietly, his voice trembling with emotion. "Not like this."

Simon's gaze softened, and he sighed deeply. "I know your heart, my son. You want justice. But justice won't come from us. Not now, not like this."

The room fell silent, the only sound crackling of the fire. Judas stared at the flickering flames, his father's words weighing heavily on him. He hated the truth in them, even as they gnawed at his resolve.

Later that night, Judas stood outside their home, staring up at the stars. The air was cool, and the village was quiet, save for the occasional bark of a dog or the murmur of distant voices. He felt a hand on his shoulder and turned to see his mother, her face gentle and understanding.

"You have your father's fire," she said softly. "But his fear, too. He only wants to protect you."

Judas shook his head. "I don't want protection. I want change. I want freedom."

"And what will you do to find it?" she asked, her voice calm but probing.

Judas didn't answer immediately. He looked away, his jaw tightening. "Something has to give. This can't go on forever."

She smiled faintly, though her eyes were sad. "Change comes in many forms, my son. Sometimes, it's not the way we expect."

He met her gaze, searching for understanding. "And if it doesn't come at all?"

"Then we endure," she said, brushing a strand of hair from his face. "Because hope is all we have left."

Judas turned back to the stars, her words lingering in his mind. He felt the weight of their reality pressing down on him but also the flicker of something else—a spark, faint but insistent, that refused to be extinguished.

CHAPTER 2: THE MARKETPLACE ENCOUNTER

The morning sunbathed the market square in a pale, golden light, but the air was heavy with tension. Judas Iscariot maneuvered through the crowded streets of Kerioth, the woven basket slung over his arm bouncing lightly against his hip. Around him, merchants called out half-heartedly, their voices muted compared to the oppressive shouts of Roman soldiers patrolling the perimeter. The metallic clink of armor and the sharp tap of boots against cobblestones were constant reminders of Rome's presence.

Judas paused at a stall laden with ripe figs. He selected a few, weighing them in his hands. The merchant, a wiry man with tired eyes, barely managed a smile as he wrapped the fruit in cloth.

"How much?" Judas asked.

The merchant hesitated, glancing nervously over Judas's shoulder. "Two denarii."

Judas frowned. "Two? Last week, it was one."

The merchant's voice dropped to a whisper. "Taxes. They increased again. I can't afford to keep my stall open otherwise."

Before Judas could respond, a commotion broke out nearby. His gaze shifted to the center of the square, where a Roman tax collector stood flanked by two soldiers. A merchant knelt before him, his face pale and his hands trembling as he held out a small leather pouch.

"This is all I have," the merchant pleaded, his voice cracking. "Please, my family is starving."

The tax collector opened the pouch, his lips curling into a sneer as he poured a paltry amount of coins into his hand. "This is an insult," he said coldly. "You owe three times this amount."

"I can't!" the merchant cried. "Please, I—"

Before he could finish, one of the soldiers stepped forward and struck him across the face with the hilt of his sword. The merchant fell to the ground, blood streaming from his nose. Gasps rippled through the crowd, but no one moved to intervene.

Judas's jaw tightened as anger surged through him. He stepped forward instinctively, his fists clenching, but a hand grabbed his arm. He turned to see an older man, his face etched with worry.

"Don't," the man whispered urgently. "You'll only make it worse."

Judas wrenched his arm free. "It's already worse," he snapped.

He marched toward the tax collector, his steps firm. Before he could reach him, the merchant on the ground grasped Judas's ankle.

"Don't," the merchant gasped, his voice barely audible. "You'll bring them down on all of us."

Judas froze, his body trembling with unspent rage. Slowly, he stepped back, his chest heaving. The soldiers smirked as they dragged the injured merchant away, leaving the crowd to disperse in tense silence.

Later that day, Judas stood near the outskirts of the market, staring at the horizon. He felt a presence beside him and turned to see a familiar figure—Lazar, a man from the village who had grown wealthy through his work as a tax collector for the Romans. Lazar's robes were fine, his sandals gleaming. He carried himself with an air of confidence that Judas found infuriating.

"You're far too tense, Judas," Lazar said with a smirk. "You'll wear yourself out carrying the burdens of the world on your shoulders."

Judas glared at him. "And you carry nothing. Not even your own dignity."

Lazar laughed, a hollow sound. "Dignity doesn't feed a family or keep a roof over their heads. I provide for mine. Can you say the same?"

"You provide by taking from your own people," Judas shot back. "You call it survival. I call it betrayal."

Lazar's expression darkened. "You speak of betrayal, but what good do your ideals bring? Do they fill bellies? Do they protect the weak? No. Ideals are worthless without power, Judas. And power belongs to those willing to take it."

Judas stepped closer, his voice low and venomous. "Power built on the backs of your own people is no power at all. It's cowardice. It's corruption."

For a moment, the two men stared at each other, the air between them crackling with tension. Then Lazar smiled, but it didn't reach his eyes.

"You'll learn, Judas," he said softly. "Sooner or later, you'll learn that the world doesn't reward those who fight for justice. It rewards those who know how to bend."

He turned and walked away, leaving Judas alone with his thoughts. The market buzzed faintly in the distance, a backdrop to the storm brewing in his heart.

That evening, Judas returned home. The day's events replayed in his mind as he sat at the table, staring at the untouched bread before him. His father's voice broke the silence.

"What happened today?" Simon asked, his tone cautious.

Judas hesitated. "I saw a man beaten for not paying his taxes. And Lazar…he was there, as smug as ever."

Simon sighed, his shoulders sagging. "Lazar made his choice. It's not our place to judge him."

"Not our place?" Judas's voice rose, his anger bubbling to the surface. "He betrays his own people, and we're supposed to stay silent? How much more must we endure before we fight back?"

Simon's gaze was steady but weary. "Fight back with what, Judas? With words? With empty hands? Rome will crush us. They always do."

"Then let them crush me," Judas said fiercely. "At least I won't bow to them."

His father shook his head, his expression a mix of frustration and sorrow. "You think defiance makes you strong, but it doesn't. Strength is knowing when to endure and when to act. You haven't learned that yet."

Judas pushed back his chair and stood; his fists clenched. "Maybe I never will. Maybe I'm tired of enduring."

He stormed out of the house, the night air cool against his flushed skin. As he walked through the quiet streets, his mother's words from the night before echoed in his mind: *Change comes in many forms, my son. Sometimes, it's not the way we expect.*

Judas looked up at the stars, his heart heavy with questions and his soul burning with unrest. Something had to change. It was a certainty that gripped him like a vice. But how, and at what cost? For now, there were no answers—only the relentless fire that refused to be extinguished.

CHAPTER 3: A FRIEND LOST

The streets of Kerioth were eerily quiet, the weight of impending tragedy hanging heavy in the air. Judas walked briskly toward the outskirts of the village, his heart pounding against his ribs. The news had reached him only minutes ago: Ezra, his closest friend since childhood, had been arrested by Roman soldiers for smuggling goods to avoid taxes. Judas's mind raced as he considered what little he could do. But doing nothing was unthinkable.

Ezra's home was a modest stone structure surrounded by a small garden. As Judas approached, he saw Ezra's wife, Miriam, standing in the doorway, clutching their infant son to her chest. Her face was pale, her eyes rimmed with red.

"Miriam," Judas called, his voice trembling. "Where is he?"

She stepped forward, her voice breaking as she spoke. "They took him to the garrison. They said he…" Her voice faltered, and she shook her head, unable to continue.

"I'll get him out," Judas said firmly, though his own doubts gnawed at him. "Stay here. I'll bring him back."

Miriam grabbed his arm. "Judas, please. Don't do anything foolish. They… they'll kill him if they think you're interfering."

He gently pried her fingers loose. "I won't let them take him. Not without a fight."

The Roman garrison loomed ahead, a cold, unyielding fortress of stone and iron. Judas approached cautiously, the weight of a small pouch of coins pressing against his side. The guards at the gate stood stiffly, their expressions unreadable.

"I need to speak to your captain," Judas said, forcing his voice to remain steady.

One of the guards stepped forward, his hand resting on the hilt of his sword. "What business do you have?"

Judas reached into his pouch and withdrew a handful of silver coins. "My friend was taken. I... I want to pay his debt. Please."

The guard glanced at the coins, then at Judas, his eyes narrowing. "Wait here."

As the guard disappeared into the garrison, Judas's pulse quickened. Minutes felt like hours before the captain emerged, his armor gleaming in the fading sunlight. He studied Judas with cold curiosity.

"You're here for the smuggler?" the captain asked, his voice clipped.

"Yes," Judas replied. "Take this. It's all I have. Just let him go."

The captain's lips curled into a smirk. "Do you think Rome is so easily bought? The punishment for smuggling is death. Your silver won't change that."

Judas's hands clenched into fists. "He has a family. A wife. A child. Please, he doesn't deserve this."

The captain's gaze hardened. "Deserve? Rome does not concern itself with what men deserve. Justice is served through order, and order demands obedience."

Before Judas could respond, the captain turned and disappeared back into the garrison. The gate slammed shut, leaving Judas standing alone, his chest heaving with frustration and despair.

Hours later, Judas sat on a hillside overlooking the village, his head in his hands. The sun had set, and the stars blinked faintly in the night sky. In the distance, he heard the faint toll of a bell—the signal of an execution. His stomach turned as realization sank in.

Footsteps approached behind him, and he turned to see Miriam, her face stricken with grief. She sank to her knees beside him, clutching his arm.

"They killed him, didn't they?" she whispered.

Judas nodded; his throat too tight to speak. Miriam sobbed, her tears soaking into his tunic. He placed a hand on her shoulder, his own eyes burning with unshed tears.

"I... I tried," he said hoarsely. "I tried to save him. But they wouldn't listen."

Miriam pulled back; her expression fierce despite her tears. "Why did you try? You knew it was hopeless. Why did you give me hope?"

Judas recoiled as if struck. "Because I couldn't do nothing. I couldn't just... stand by."

She shook her head, her voice rising. "And now my son has no father. My husband is dead. And nothing has changed."

Her words pierced him like a blade. Miriam turned and walked away, leaving Judas alone under the vast, indifferent sky.

That night, Judas returned home. The house was dark and silent, his parents already asleep. He sat at the table, staring at the cold remains of the evening meal. His father's words from days before echoed in his mind: *Strength is knowing when to endure and when to act.*

A surge of anger coursed through him, and he slammed his fist against the table. "If God is with us," he muttered bitterly, "where was He for Ezra?"

The silence that followed was deafening. Judas buried his head in his hands, the weight of his grief and guilt threatening to crush him.

In the days that followed, Judas avoided the marketplace and the familiar faces of the village. He wandered the outskirts of Kerioth, his thoughts a chaotic swirl of anger and despair. The memory of Ezra's laughter, his easy smile, haunted him. He thought of the plans they'd made as boys, their dreams of a better world. All of it was gone now, snuffed out like a candle in the wind.

One afternoon, as he sat by a stream, he heard footsteps approaching. A stranger emerged from the trees; his robes simple but clean. The man's eyes were kind, yet piercing, as if he could see the turmoil within Judas.

"You carry a heavy burden," the stranger said.

Judas scoffed. "What would you know of it?"

The man smiled faintly. "More than you might think. But burdens are not meant to be carried alone."

Judas frowned. "Who are you?"

"A traveler," the man replied. "And perhaps… a guide."

The cryptic words only deepened Judas's frustration. "There is no guide for this," he said bitterly. "My friend is dead. Killed by men who care nothing for justice. Tell me, traveler, what guide can bring meaning to that?"

The man regarded him quietly for a moment before speaking. "Perhaps it is not meaning you seek, but purpose. And purpose, my friend, is rarely found in answers. It is found in action."

Judas looked away, his thoughts churning. The man's words lingered long after he had gone, echoing in Judas's mind as he stared into the rippling waters of the stream.

CHAPTER 4: THE SPARK OF REBELLION

The room was dimly lit by a single oil lamp, casting flickering shadows on the rough stone walls. The air was thick with the scent of sweat and damp earth. Judas Iscariot leaned against the doorframe, arms crossed, his gaze fixed on the men gathered around the wooden table in the center. Their voices were low, urgent, and filled with barely contained fury.

"Rome bleeds us dry," one man said, his fist pounding the table for emphasis. "If we do nothing, they'll take everything. Our crops, our homes, our families."

"And what do you propose?" another asked, his tone skeptical. "March into the garrison with pitchforks? They'll cut us down before we reach the gate."

"No," the first man said, leaning forward. His eyes burned with determination. "We strike where they least expect it. A caravan here, a patrol there. We hit them hard, and we disappear before they can retaliate."

Murmurs of agreement rippled through the group, but Judas remained silent. He recognized the speaker, a zealot named Baruch, whose fiery rhetoric had drawn many to their cause. But something about the plan gnawed at Judas's conscience.

"And what then?" Judas finally spoke, his voice cutting through the noise. The men turned to look at him. "We kill a few soldiers, disrupt a caravan. What does that achieve? Rome will send more soldiers, more punishment. It'll be our families who pay the price."

Baruch's eyes narrowed. "So, we do nothing? We sit back and let them grind us into the dirt?"

"No," Judas said, his voice steady but firm. "But this... this isn't a solution. Killing a few soldiers won't free us. It will bury us."

The room fell silent, the tension palpable. Finally, a younger zealot, barely more than a boy, spoke up, his voice tinged with defiance. "You're all talk, Judas. Always questioning, always doubting. Maybe you don't have the stomach for what needs to be done."

Judas's jaw tightened, but he didn't rise to the bait. Instead, he stepped forward, his gaze sweeping across the room. "I want freedom as much as any of you. But freedom doesn't come from reckless violence. It comes from unity, from strategy. This... this is desperation masquerading as rebellion."

Baruch stood, his expression hard. "We don't need your approval, Judas. If you're not willing to fight, then step aside. But don't stand in our way."

Judas met his gaze, unflinching. "I'm not standing in your way. I'm trying to save you from yourselves."

The room erupted in murmurs again, but Judas didn't wait to hear more. He turned and walked out into the cool night air, his thoughts a storm of frustration and doubt.

Judas's footsteps echoed on the cobblestone path as he made his way back toward the village. The stars above were sharp and cold, their light offering little comfort. He couldn't shake the image of Baruch's burning eyes, the boy's taunt ringing in his ears.

"Maybe you don't have the stomach for what needs to be done."

Was it true? Did he lack the courage to fight? Or was he the only one who saw the futility of their path? The questions gnawed at him, their weight pressing down on his chest.

As he approached the outskirts of the village, a familiar voice called out. "Judas."

He turned to see his father, Simon, standing by the well. The older man's face was lined with worry, his eyes searching.

"Where have you been?" Simon asked, his voice low but firm.

Judas hesitated, then sighed. "Talking to Baruch and his men. They... they want to strike back against Rome. Attack their soldiers, their supply lines."

Simon's expression darkened. "And you? Do you want that too?"

"I don't know," Judas admitted. "Part of me admires their courage. But their plan... it's reckless. It'll bring nothing but more suffering."

Simon stepped closer, placing a hand on Judas's shoulder. "Courage without wisdom is a dangerous thing, my son. You're right to question them. But remember, inaction has its own cost. The challenge is finding the path that brings true change."

Judas looked away, his jaw tightening. "What if there is no path, Father? What if we're just... trapped?"

Simon's hand tightened briefly before releasing him. "Trapped or not, we must choose how we face it. With anger, with fear, or with purpose. That choice is ours, no matter the circumstances."

The following morning, Judas found himself wandering the outskirts of Kerioth again, his mind still churning. He came across a small clearing where a group of children played, their laughter a stark contrast to the heaviness that weighed on him. He stopped, watching as they chased each other, their innocence untouched by the struggles of the world around them.

"A rare sight, isn't it?" a voice said behind him.

Judas turned to see a man standing there, his robes simple but clean. The stranger from the stream. The man's expression was calm, but his eyes held a quiet intensity.

"You again," Judas said, his tone wary. "What do you want?"

The man smiled faintly. "To offer a different perspective. You're at a crossroads, Judas. I can see it in your eyes."

Judas frowned. "You think you know me?"

"I know the weight of doubt," the man said. "And the fire of anger. Both can consume you if you're not careful."

Judas crossed his arms. "And what do you suggest? That I sit back and do nothing? Let Rome continue to crush us?"

The man shook his head. "No. But action without purpose is as dangerous as inaction. The question isn't whether to act. It's how."

Judas stared at him, his mind racing. Finally, he asked, "Who are you?"

The man's smile widened slightly, but he didn't answer. Instead, he turned and walked away, leaving Judas standing alone in the clearing. The children's laughter faded into the distance as the weight of the man's words settled over him.

That night, Judas sat alone under the stars, the flickering light of a small fire illuminating his face. His thoughts were a tangled web of anger, doubt, and determination. He could still hear Baruch's voice, see Simon's steady gaze, feel the stranger's quiet intensity.

He reached into his tunic and pulled out a small coin, turning it over in his fingers. It caught the firelight, its surface gleaming like a distant star. For the first time, he allowed himself to consider the possibility that his path might not lie with Baruch or the zealots. But where it would lead, he couldn't yet see.

The fire crackled softly, and Judas closed his eyes, the weight of his choices pressing down on him. The spark of rebellion burned within him, but it was no longer a simple flame. It was a question, a challenge, and a call to something greater—something he couldn't yet name.

CHAPTER 5: THE QUIET VOICE

The market hummed with life, a cacophony of voices rising and falling like the tide. Merchants called out their wares, the aroma of spices and freshly baked bread mingling with the less savory scent of livestock. Judas moved through the crowd with practiced ease, his basket empty save for a few coins jingling at the bottom. Today, he was here not for goods but for distraction. The events of the past days had weighed heavily on him, and the market's bustle offered a temporary reprieve.

As he paused at a stall selling dates, he overheard a conversation nearby. A man with a soft but resonant voice was speaking, and his words caught Judas's attention.

"There is a teacher in Galilee," the man said, his tone calm but insistent. "They say he speaks of a new kingdom, not of power or swords, but of love and forgiveness."

Judas turned toward the speaker, a thin, weathered man whose robes were patched but clean. He stood amidst a small group of listeners, his hands gesturing as he spoke. Intrigued, Judas edged closer.

"Forgiveness?" a skeptical voice from the crowd asked. "Against Rome? That's not salvation; that's surrender."

The man smiled faintly; his expression unruffled. "Is it? Or is it the beginning of something greater? The teacher says that true strength lies not in striking back, but in turning the other cheek. That love is more powerful than hate."

Judas frowned, his curiosity battling with his instinctive doubt.

He stepped forward, his voice cutting through the murmurs. "And what does love do when soldiers march into your village? When they take your food, your friends, your lives? Does it stop their swords?"

The man met his gaze, unflinching. "It may not stop their swords, but it can stop you from becoming like them. Hate is a poison that destroys the vessel as surely as the target."

Judas's fists clenched at his sides. "And what does that achieve? Survival? Submission? A life spent bowing to those who would see us crushed?"

"Perhaps," the man said softly, "we've been fighting the wrong battle. Perhaps the kingdom this teacher speaks of is not of this world."

The crowd murmured, some nodding in agreement, others scoffing. Judas's mind churned with conflicting emotions. He wanted to dismiss the man's words as naive, but something about his calm conviction held him in place.

Later, as the crowd began to disperse, Judas approached the man, his steps purposeful. "This teacher you speak of," he began, "who is he?"

The man regarded him with a curious expression. "His name is Jesus of Nazareth. He preaches in Galilee, though his words have begun to spread far beyond."

Judas hesitated. "And you believe him?"

The man smiled. "I've seen the way his words change people. The way they heal wounds that swords cannot. I believe there is power in that."

Judas's jaw tightened. "Words won't drive Rome from our land. They won't bring back the dead."

"No," the man agreed. "But perhaps they can stop more from dying."

Judas turned away, his thoughts a whirlwind. He had heard of this

Jesus before, in passing whispers and fragmented stories. A man who healed the sick, who preached of a kingdom not of this earth. But he had dismissed such tales as fantasies, distractions from the harsh reality of their lives. Now, though, he found himself unable to shake the stranger's words.

That evening, Judas sat by the fire outside his home, the flames casting dancing shadows on his face. His father, Simon, joined him, settling onto a low stool with a groan.

"You've been quiet," Simon said, breaking the silence. "Something on your mind?"

Judas poked at the fire with a stick, his gaze distant. "I heard about a man today. A teacher from Galilee. They say he speaks of love and forgiveness as the path to salvation."

Simon raised an eyebrow. "And what do you think of that?"

Judas's lips pressed into a thin line. "I think it's foolish. Forgiveness won't drive out the Romans. It won't feed the hungry or protect the weak."

"Perhaps not," Simon said slowly. "But perhaps it's not meant to. Sometimes, salvation isn't about changing the world. Sometimes, it's about changing ourselves."

Judas looked at his father sharply. "And what good does that do if the world remains the same? If we're still crushed under Rome's heel?"

Simon sighed; his gaze fixed on the fire. "I don't have the answers, Judas. But I do know this: hate consumes. And if you let it, it will consume you, too."

Judas said nothing, the flickering flames reflecting in his dark eyes.

The following day, Judas returned to the marketplace, scanning the crowd for the stranger. He found him near the well, speaking to a small group of villagers. This time, Judas stayed on the fringes, listening without interruption.

The man spoke of hope, of a kingdom where the weary would find rest and the oppressed would be free. He spoke of a teacher who challenged power not with violence but with truth. His words painted a picture of a world Judas could scarcely imagine, one where love was stronger than hate, where forgiveness held more power than revenge.

As the group began to disperse, Judas stepped forward, his skepticism warring with his curiosity. "Where can I find this Jesus?" he asked.

The man's eyes met his, steady and kind. "He often teaches near the Sea of Galilee. If you seek him, you will find him."

Judas nodded, his thoughts swirling. He wasn't sure why he asked, why he cared. But the stranger's words had planted a seed, one that refused to be ignored.

That night, as Judas lay on his mat, sleep eluded him. His mind replayed the stranger's words, his descriptions of Jesus and his teachings. Part of him wanted to dismiss it all as foolishness. Another part, however small, whispered that there might be something there worth exploring.

As the stars wheeled overhead, Judas stared into the darkness, his heart torn between doubt and a faint, fragile hope. He did not know what he would do next, but for the first time in days, he felt the stirrings of something other than anger—a quiet voice, urging him to listen.

CHAPTER 6: THE MEETING

The hills near the Sea of Galilee were alive with the murmur of a gathered crowd. The sun hung high in the sky, its light shimmering on the waves of the lake below. Judas approached cautiously, weaving his way through clusters of people. Some were seated on the ground, others stood, craning their necks for a better view of the man at the center of it all.

Jesus of Nazareth.

Judas had heard whispers of him for weeks, but now, here he was, face-to-face with the mystery. Well, not quite face-to-face. He still stood at the edge of the throng, hesitant to push forward. The man at the center of the crowd sat on a low hill, speaking in a voice that carried like a melody on the breeze.

"Blessed are the poor in spirit," Jesus said, his tone gentle but firm, "for theirs is the kingdom of heaven. Blessed are those who mourn, for they will be comforted."

Judas stopped in his tracks, the words washing over him like waves. They were simple, yet they seemed to burrow into his chest, stirring something he couldn't quite name. He shook his head, trying to dismiss the feeling.

"Foolishness," he muttered under his breath, but his feet carried him closer.

The crowd hung on every word. Women with babies at their breasts, men with sun-beaten faces, children fidgeting in the dust—all were riveted. Judas caught snippets of their murmured reactions:

"Did you hear that?"

"He speaks as if he truly knows us."

"Such wisdom… such love."

Judas scoffed, though he wasn't sure if it was at the words or at himself for lingering. He folded his arms, his expression guarded as he listened.

"Blessed are the peacemakers, for they will be called children of God," Jesus continued, his eyes scanning the crowd. "You have heard that it was said, 'An eye for an eye, and a tooth for a tooth.' But I tell you, do not resist an evil person. If anyone slaps you on the right cheek, turn to them the other cheek also."

Judas felt his stomach twist. Turning the other cheek? He clenched his fists at his sides, his mind flashing to the Roman soldiers who had humiliated his neighbors, beaten his friends, and murdered Ezra. Could Jesus truly believe that submission was the answer?

The sermon continued, but Judas's thoughts were loud in his ears, drowning out parts of Jesus's words. Then, just as he was about to step away, Jesus turned his gaze toward him. Judas froze. There was no mistaking it. Jesus's eyes found his in the sea of faces, and for a moment, Judas felt as if he were utterly exposed.

"Come to me, all you who are weary and burdened, and I will give you rest," Jesus said, and though the words were meant for the crowd, Judas felt them pierce his very soul.

After the sermon, the crowd began to disperse, many lingering to speak with Jesus or with one another. Judas stayed back, his heart pounding. He told himself he was merely curious, nothing more. But his feet moved toward the man who had held the crowd's attention so effortlessly.

Jesus stood near the edge of the hill, speaking with a small group. His presence was calm, unhurried, as if time itself slowed in his company. Judas lingered nearby, unsure of how to approach.

Then Jesus turned, his gaze meeting Judas's once more. This time, he smiled and gestured for him to come closer. Judas hesitated, then stepped forward, his jaw tight and his shoulders squared.

"You are troubled," Jesus said, his voice quiet but certain.

Judas stopped short, his lips pressing into a thin line. "Am I?" he replied, his tone sharper than he intended.

Jesus's smile didn't waver. "You carry the weight of the world, Judas. But is it yours to bear?"

The question hung in the air, striking Judas like a blow. He stared at Jesus, searching for any trace of mockery, but found none. There was only a quiet understanding that both comforted and unnerved him.

"If we don't bear it, who will?" Judas asked, his voice low but charged.

"Perhaps," Jesus said, "it is not about bearing the weight, but about learning where to lay it down."

Judas's brow furrowed. "And where would that be? At the feet of Rome? At the mercy of those who oppress us?"

Jesus stepped closer; his expression serious but kind. "Not at the feet of Rome, but at the feet of God. True freedom, Judas, is not found in rebellion or submission. It is found in the peace that surpasses understanding."

The words stirred something deep within Judas, but he fought against it. "Easy words," he said bitterly. "But words won't free our people. Words won't bring back the dead."

"No," Jesus agreed. "But they might stop more from dying."

Judas looked away; his chest tight. He wanted to argue, to push back, but he found himself at a loss. For a long moment, the two stood in silence, the murmurs of the dispersing crowd fading into the background.

"You see the brokenness of the world clearly," Jesus said finally. "That is a gift, but also a burden. Come with me, Judas. Walk with me. Perhaps together we can find what you seek."

Judas's gaze snapped back to Jesus, startled. "You don't even know me."

"But I know your heart," Jesus replied.

Judas opened his mouth to respond, but no words came. Instead, he nodded, a silent agreement born of curiosity and something he could not yet name.

As the sun dipped lower in the sky, Judas walked with Jesus and the small group of followers who had stayed behind. They spoke of many things—of the kingdom Jesus preached, of the struggles they faced, of the hope that seemed so elusive. Judas listened more than he spoke, his mind churning with questions.

That night, as they made camp by the lake, Judas sat apart from the others, staring into the flames of the fire. Jesus approached, settling beside him without a word. For a long time, they sat in silence, the crackling fire the only sound.

Finally, Jesus spoke. "Do you believe in hope, Judas?"

Judas's lips twitched into a faint, humorless smile. "I want to. But it's hard to find."

"Perhaps it's not something to be found," Jesus said. "Perhaps it's something to be created."

Judas turned to look at him, his skepticism warring with the faint stirrings of hope. For the first time in years, he felt the weight on his shoulders lighten, if only slightly. He didn't know where this path would lead, but for now, he was willing to follow.

And for the first time, the quiet voice in his heart grew just a little louder.

CHAPTER 7: JOINING THE DISCIPLES

The air was thick with the salty tang of the Sea of Galilee, a breeze rippling through the small camp where Jesus and his followers had settled for the evening. Judas stood at the edge of the gathering, his arms crossed over his chest, observing the disciples as they went about their tasks. A fire crackled at the center, illuminating their faces in soft, flickering light.

He wasn't sure why he'd stayed. He'd listened to Jesus speak earlier in the day, his words cutting through the noise of doubt in Judas's mind. Yet even as hope stirred faintly within him, skepticism lingered. These men seemed too idealistic, too certain that words and love could stand against the might of Rome. And yet, here he was.

"Judas," a voice called, startling him. He turned to see Jesus approaching, his steps unhurried, his expression open and warm. "Come, sit with us."

Judas hesitated, then nodded, following Jesus to the fire. The other disciples greeted him with wary glances, their conversations stuttering to a halt. He felt their eyes on him, weighing and judging.

Peter, seated closest to Jesus, spoke first. "Who is this?" he asked bluntly, his gaze sharp.

"Judas Iscariot," Jesus replied, taking a seat on a low stone. "A man with much to offer."

Peter raised an eyebrow, his skepticism clear. "He doesn't look like someone who's here for faith."

Judas's jaw tightened, but he kept his voice even. "And what does someone here for faith look like?"

Peter's eyes narrowed. "Someone who doesn't question everything."

Jesus intervened with a calm smile. "Faith without questions is blind, Peter. And questions often lead us closer to truth."

Judas felt a flicker of gratitude but kept his expression neutral. "I'm not here to disrupt," he said. "I'm here because I need to know if there's more than what I've seen. More than… this." He gestured vaguely, encompassing the oppressive world they lived in.

Andrew, seated beside Peter, frowned. "And what is it you hope to find?"

Judas hesitated, then spoke honestly. "A way forward. Something better than violence but stronger than submission. Something real."

The fire popped, sending a spray of sparks into the air. The group fell silent, each man lost in his own thoughts. Finally, Jesus spoke.

"You will find what you seek here, Judas," he said. "But it will not come easily. The path ahead is narrow, and it requires more than strength. It requires trust."

Judas met his gaze, feeling the weight of the words. "Trust is earned," he said quietly.

Jesus inclined his head. "Then let us earn it."

Over the next few days, Judas traveled with the disciples, observing their routines and listening to their conversations. He noticed the camaraderie among them, though it often felt strained. Peter, in particular, seemed to keep a close eye on him, as if waiting for Judas to reveal some hidden agenda.

One afternoon, as they rested beneath the shade of an olive tree, Judas found himself seated beside Peter. The silence between them was tense, and Judas finally broke it.

"You don't trust me," he said, not as a question but as a statement.

Peter didn't deny it. "You're right. I don't."

Judas smirked faintly. "At least you're honest."

Peter's gaze didn't waver. "You question everything. Is that faith?"

Judas turned to him; his expression serious. "If I don't question, how can I know what's true?"

Peter considered this for a moment, then nodded grudgingly. "Maybe. But questions can also lead you astray. Be careful, Judas. Doubt is a heavy burden."

Judas didn't respond, his thoughts churning. He couldn't deny the truth in Peter's words, but neither could he ignore the restless need for answers that drove him.

That evening, as the group shared a modest meal, Judas found himself drawn into conversation with John, the youngest of the disciples. Unlike Peter, John seemed open and curious, his questions more about understanding than judgment.

"What brought you here?" John asked, his voice soft but earnest.

Judas hesitated. "I've seen too much suffering," he said finally. "Too much hate. I don't know if I believe in what Jesus preaches, but… I want to. I want to believe there's another way."

John smiled. "That's enough. Belief doesn't always come all at once. Sometimes, it grows slowly, like a seed."

Judas tilted his head, studying him. "You seem certain of your faith. How did you find it?"

John's gaze grew distant. "I listened. I watched. And I saw how Jesus's words changed people—not just their minds, but their hearts. It's hard to explain, but when you see it, you'll understand."

Judas's lips twitched into a faint smile. "You make it sound so simple."

"It's not," John said with a laugh. "But it is worth it."

As the days turned into weeks, Judas began to feel a tentative sense of belonging. He still clashed with Peter, whose brusque nature grated against his own, but he found allies in John's gentle curiosity and Andrew's quiet pragmatism. Most of all, he found himself drawn to Jesus, whose patience and understanding seemed boundless.

One evening, as the group prepared to move to another village, Judas approached Jesus. The two walked a short distance from the others, the setting sun painting the sky in hues of gold and crimson.

"Why did you ask me to follow you?" Judas asked, his voice low.

Jesus looked at him, his expression thoughtful. "Because I saw your heart. You have a fire within you, Judas. It burns for justice, for truth. That fire can destroy, or it can illuminate. The choice is yours."

Judas frowned, the words both comforting and unsettling. "And what if I make the wrong choice?"

"Then you will learn," Jesus said simply. "And you will grow. The journey is as important as the destination."

For a long moment, they walked in silence, the sound of their footsteps mingling with the distant calls of birds. Judas felt the weight of his doubts and questions, but for the first time, he also felt the faint stirrings of hope—a fragile thing, but real nonetheless.

"I'll try," he said finally.

Jesus smiled. "That is all I ask."

CHAPTER 8: MIRACLES AND QUESTIONS

The sun bore down on the hills of Judea, its heat shimmering in the air as the crowd gathered around Jesus. The sound of murmurs and quiet awe rippled through the masses as a blind man stumbled forward, led by a younger woman who whispered in his ear. Judas stood on the outskirts, his arms folded, his expression guarded as he watched the scene unfold.

Jesus stepped forward, his presence calm yet commanding. He gently placed his hands on the man's shoulders, speaking softly. Though Judas couldn't hear the words, he saw the blind man's face shift from apprehension to something that looked like hope. Moments later, the man's eyes opened, clear and bright, and he gasped, tears streaming down his cheeks.

"I can see!" the man exclaimed, his voice breaking with emotion. "I can see!"

The crowd erupted into cheers and cries of wonder. People surged forward, their hands reaching out to Jesus as if his touch alone could heal their wounds, their pain. Judas felt the energy around him, a mixture of hope and desperation, and he couldn't deny the power of the moment.

Yet, a seed of doubt lingered. He leaned closer to John, who stood beside him, his young face alight with admiration.

"It's incredible," John murmured, his voice full of reverence. "Did you see the joy on his face?"

Judas nodded slowly. "I saw it. But what does it change?"

John turned to him, puzzled. "What do you mean?"

"One man can see again," Judas said, his voice low. "But what about the rest? What about the soldiers who take what isn't theirs? The taxes that leave families starving? Healing one man doesn't free the rest of us."

John frowned but didn't respond. Judas didn't press the matter. He turned his attention back to the crowd, watching as Jesus continued to move among them, his touch bringing comfort, his words offering peace.

Later that evening, the disciples gathered around a fire, their conversations lively as they recounted the day's events. Judas sat on the edge of the group, listening as Peter spoke animatedly.

"Did you see the boy with the withered hand?" Peter said, his voice rising with excitement. "One touch, and it was as if he'd never been hurt. It's a miracle, plain and simple."

Andrew nodded, his expression thoughtful. "It's more than that. It's a sign. People are starting to believe."

Judas's brow furrowed. "Believe in what?"

The group fell quiet, their eyes turning to him. Peter's smile faded, replaced by a look of irritation.

"In the kingdom," Peter said firmly. "In what Jesus is bringing."

Judas met his gaze, unflinching. "And what is that, exactly? Feeding the hungry? Healing the sick? Compassion feeds the hungry, but it doesn't free the oppressed."

Peter's jaw tightened, but before he could respond, Jesus spoke from the other side of the fire.

"It is both," Jesus said, his voice calm but carrying authority. The disciples turned to him, their attention fully captured. "Compassion is the beginning of freedom. It shows people they are seen, that they are loved. Without that, no kingdom can stand."

Judas frowned. "But it doesn't change the laws. It doesn't stop the soldiers. How does it bring liberation?"

Jesus's gaze rested on Judas; his expression unreadable. "Tell me, Judas, what do you believe liberation looks like?"

Judas hesitated. "Justice. Fairness. An end to the suffering we've endured for generations."

"And how would you bring it?" Jesus asked.

Judas's fists clenched. "Sometimes, you have to fight. Rome doesn't care about compassion. They understand power, and nothing else."

Jesus nodded slowly; his gaze unwavering. "And when the fighting is done, what then? Will the sword bring peace? Or will it sow seeds for more violence?"

The fire crackled, the silence stretching as the weight of the question settled over them. Judas looked away, his thoughts churning.

Later, as the others drifted off to sleep, Judas approached Jesus, who sat alone at the edge of the camp, gazing at the stars. He hesitated, then lowered himself to the ground beside him.

"You frustrate me," Judas admitted, his voice quiet but intense.

Jesus chuckled softly. "I've been told that before."

Judas sighed, running a hand through his hair. "I don't understand you. You have this… power. You could do so much more with it. You could lead us to real freedom."

"And what is real freedom, Judas?" Jesus asked, turning to look at him.

Judas gestured vaguely, his frustration mounting. "Freedom from Rome. From fear. From hunger."

Jesus's gaze softened. "And if I give people bread, will they not hunger again? If I drive out Rome, will another oppressor not take its place? True freedom is not found in the absence of suffering, but in the presence of peace—peace within the heart."

Judas shook his head. "That sounds like surrender."

"It is trust," Jesus corrected gently. "Trust in something greater than ourselves. Greater than Rome, greater than any kingdom on earth."

Judas fell silent, staring out at the dark expanse of the hills. The words unsettled him, yet they also stirred something deep within, a longing he couldn't quite name.

"I want to believe you," he said finally. "But it's hard. Every part of me screams that it's not enough."

"That is the struggle of faith," Jesus said. "To trust, even when it seems impossible. To see beyond what is and believe in what could be."

Judas turned to him, searching his face for answers he knew he wouldn't find. "And what if I can't?"

Jesus placed a hand on his shoulder, his touch steady and reassuring. "Then you will keep walking, and I will walk with you."

In the days that followed, Judas continued to watch and question. He saw Jesus heal the sick, feed the hungry, and speak words that brought hope to the hopeless. Each act left him awed, yet his doubts remained, an ever-present shadow.

But he also began to notice something else. The people Jesus touched didn't just walk away healed; they walked away changed. Their eyes shone with a light that hadn't been there before, a spark of something deeper than physical relief. It was as if Jesus had given them not just healing, but a reason to hope.

And though Judas couldn't yet name it, that spark began to take root within him as well.

CHAPTER 9: SIGNS OF DIVISION

The campfire crackled softly as the disciples gathered around it, their faces illuminated by its flickering light. The day had been long, filled with walking and teaching in the villages. Yet, as the night settled, the atmosphere around the fire was anything but peaceful. Tensions simmered, bubbling beneath the surface like water threatening to boil over.

"We can't keep ignoring the bigger picture," Judas said, his voice cutting through the low murmur of conversation. He leaned forward, his gaze fixed on Peter, who sat across from him. "Healing the sick, feeding the hungry—it's good, but it's not enough. It doesn't change the fact that Rome still has its boot on our necks."

Peter's eyes narrowed. "And what would you have us do, Judas? Take up swords? March on the garrisons?"

"If that's what it takes," Judas replied, his voice hard. "Revolutions are not built on forgiveness."

The group fell silent, the weight of his words hanging in the air. Andrew shifted uncomfortably, while John glanced nervously at Jesus, who sat quietly at the edge of the circle, his gaze distant but attentive.

"You think you know better than the Teacher?" Peter challenged; his tone sharp. "You think your way is more righteous?"

"I think my way is practical," Judas shot back. "You can preach love and peace all you want, but Rome doesn't care about love. They understand power. And right now, we have none."

"Enough," Jesus said softly, his voice carrying a weight that silenced the group. He turned to Judas, his expression calm but firm. "Tell me, Judas, what does power look like to you?"

Judas hesitated, caught off guard by the question. "Power is... control. It's the ability to shape the world as it should be. To end suffering, to bring justice."

Jesus nodded slowly. "And do you believe that power comes from violence? From the sword?"

"Sometimes, yes," Judas said, his voice steady. "Sometimes, that's the only language oppressors understand."

"And when the sword has spoken," Jesus asked, "what remains? What grows from the seeds of violence?"

Judas frowned, his frustration mounting. "You speak in riddles, Jesus. Rome doesn't care about seeds or peace. They care about control. If we don't fight, we'll be crushed."

Peter crossed his arms, his expression triumphant. "And that's why you'll never understand. The Teacher's way is different. It's harder, yes, but it's the only way to truly change the world."

"Change the world?" Judas scoffed. "You can't change the world by letting your enemies walk all over you."

Jesus stood, his movements deliberate. The firelight danced across his face as he addressed the group. "The world changes not through the sword, but through the heart. Violence begets violence. Hatred breeds more hatred. But love—love transforms."

Judas opened his mouth to argue, but Jesus held up a hand. "I know your doubts, Judas. I know your frustration. And I understand it. But I ask you to trust that there is another way. A harder way, yes, but one that leads to true freedom."

The silence that followed was heavy, each disciple lost in their own thoughts. Judas stared at the fire, his jaw tight, his mind churning. He wanted to believe Jesus, wanted to trust in this vision of a better world. But he couldn't silence the voice in his head that screamed for action, for justice.

Later, as the disciples dispersed to their sleeping spots, Judas lingered by the fire. He was startled when John approached, his youthful face thoughtful.

"You're not entirely wrong, you know," John said quietly.

Judas glanced at him, surprised. "Oh? I thought everyone here believed I was the troublemaker."

John smiled faintly. "You question things. That's not a bad thing. It's just... hard for some of us to hear. Especially Peter."

Judas let out a bitter laugh. "Peter would follow Jesus off a cliff if he asked. No questions, no doubts."

"And you think that's a weakness?" John asked, his tone neutral.

"I think blind faith is dangerous," Judas said. "If you don't question, how do you know you're on the right path?"

John nodded slowly. "Maybe. But sometimes, faith isn't about having all the answers. Sometimes, it's about trusting the journey."

Judas didn't respond, his gaze fixed on the dying embers of the fire.

The following morning, the group set out early, the sun rising over the hills as they walked. Judas fell into step beside Andrew, whose quiet demeanor often made him a calming presence.

"You've been quiet," Andrew said, glancing at him.

Judas shrugged. "Just thinking."

"About what?"

Judas hesitated. "About whether this path we're on will actually lead anywhere. Or if we're just walking in circles."

Andrew chuckled softly. "Sometimes it feels that way. But then I see the way people look at Jesus, the way his words give them hope, and I think... maybe that's enough."

"Hope doesn't change laws," Judas muttered. "It doesn't free the oppressed."

Andrew sighed. "Maybe not. But it gives people strength to keep going. And sometimes, that's the first step."

Judas didn't reply, his thoughts too tangled to untangle in the moment.

That night, as they made camp, Judas approached Jesus, who was sitting alone by the water's edge. The moonlight reflected off the waves, casting a silvery glow over the scene.

"May I join you?" Judas asked.

Jesus nodded, gesturing for him to sit. For a while, neither of them spoke, the gentle lapping of the water filling the silence.

Finally, Judas broke the stillness. "Do you ever doubt?"

Jesus turned to him, his expression thoughtful. "I have moments of doubt, yes. But I also have faith. Not in the path itself, but in the One who leads me."

Judas frowned. "It's easier for you. You have this... presence, this power. People listen to you. Follow you. But the rest of us? We're just trying to survive."

Jesus reached out, placing a hand on Judas's shoulder. "You have more power than you realize, Judas. The power to choose. To believe. To love. That power can change the world more than any sword ever could."

Judas looked away, his chest tight with conflicting emotions. "I don't know if I can believe that."

"You don't have to believe it all at once," Jesus said gently. "Just take the next step. And the one after that. Trust that the path will become clearer as you walk it."

For the first time in days, Judas felt a flicker of peace. It was small, fragile, but it was enough to keep him walking.

CHAPTER 10: THE KINGDOM'S COST

The night was unusually quiet. The disciples' camp rested beneath a canopy of stars, the faint sound of crickets providing the only music of the evening. Judas sat apart from the others; his gaze fixed on the flickering flames of the campfire. His thoughts were a storm of questions, doubts, and fears—a maelstrom that seemed to intensify with every passing day.

He barely noticed Jesus approaching until he heard his quiet footsteps on the dry earth. Judas glanced up, his brow furrowed, as Jesus settled beside him. For a moment, neither spoke, the silence stretching between them like a taut thread.

"You're troubled," Jesus said at last, his voice soft but certain.

Judas gave a short laugh, though there was no humor in it. "Is it that obvious?"

Jesus's gaze was steady. "Only to those who care to look."

Judas hesitated, then sighed. "I don't understand you, Jesus. I see the way people follow you, the way your words move them. But I can't help wondering... what is all this for? What are we fighting for?"

Jesus's expression grew thoughtful. "The kingdom."

Judas frowned. "The kingdom? You speak of it often, but you never explain what it means. Is it freedom from Rome? Justice for our people? What is this kingdom you keep talking about?"

Jesus's gaze shifted to the fire, the light dancing in his eyes. "The kingdom is not of this world, Judas."

The words landed heavily, and Judas's frustration bubbled to the surface. "Then what are we fighting for?" he demanded. "If it's not about this world, if it's not about freeing our people, then what's the point?"

Jesus turned back to him, his expression calm but unyielding. "It is about freeing our people. But not in the way you think. True freedom is not found in the overthrow of Rome. It is found in the transformation of the heart."

Judas's jaw tightened. "You think the Romans care about our hearts? They care about power, about control. They don't care if we feel free inside as long as we're still under their heel."

"And if we trade one oppressor for another?" Jesus asked. "If we take power through violence, what becomes of us? What seeds do we sow for the generations to come?"

Judas looked away, his hands clenched into fists. "You speak in riddles, as if the answers are so simple. But they're not. People are suffering now. They're hungry now. They need justice now."

Jesus reached out, placing a hand on Judas's shoulder. "I know their suffering. I see it every day. But the path to true justice is not through the sword. It is through love. Through forgiveness. Through sacrifice."

The last word hung in the air, heavy with meaning. Judas turned back to Jesus, his brow furrowing. "Sacrifice?"

Jesus's gaze was distant, his voice quieter. "The kingdom comes at a cost. And that cost is great."

Judas felt a chill run through him. "What are you saying? What cost?"

Jesus didn't answer directly. Instead, he spoke as if to the stars. "A shepherd lays down his life for his sheep. Not because he must, but because he chooses to. That is love. That is the kingdom."

Judas's chest tightened, a mixture of alarm and confusion swirling within him. "You're not making sense. If you're saying what I think you're saying…" He trailed off, unable to finish the thought.

Jesus turned to him, his eyes filled with a deep, unshakable resolve. "What do you fear, Judas?"

Judas's voice rose, his frustration spilling over. "I fear that you're leading us to nothing! That all this hope you're giving people will end in ashes. That your vision of the kingdom is a dream that will die with you!"

Jesus's expression didn't change. If anything, his calm seemed to deepen. "And if it does? If the dream must die for it to take root, would it not be worth it?"

Judas stared at him, his heart pounding. "You're asking too much. You're asking us to follow you into the dark without knowing what's on the other side."

"Faith," Jesus said simply. "That is faith, Judas. Trusting in what cannot be seen. Believing in what cannot yet be understood."

Judas shook his head, standing abruptly. "I don't know if I can do that. I don't know if I can follow you blindly."

Jesus stood as well, his expression gentle but firm. "I'm not asking you to follow blindly. I'm asking you to walk with me. To see. To question. And to choose."

Judas looked away, his thoughts a whirlwind of doubt and fear. The silence stretched between them, heavy with unspoken words. Finally, he turned and walked back toward the camp, leaving Jesus alone beneath the vast expanse of the night sky.

That night, Judas lay awake, staring up at the stars. The conversation played over and over in his mind, each word a thorn that pricked at his certainty. He felt as if he were standing on the edge of a great chasm, unsure whether to leap or retreat.

In the distance, he heard the faint sound of Jesus's voice, speaking softly to someone—or perhaps to himself. Judas closed his eyes, the weight of the kingdom's cost pressing heavily on his chest. He didn't know if he could bear it. And yet, he couldn't bring himself to walk away.

Not yet.

CHAPTER 11: WHISPERS OF BETRAYAL

The moonlight bathed the courtyard of the temple in an eerie glow. Judas lingered near the edge of the stone steps, his heart pounding in his chest. He had received the message earlier that evening—an invitation, cryptic but unmistakable, to meet with the temple priests. Now, standing here, he couldn't shake the sense of foreboding that clung to him like a second skin.

"Judas," a voice called softly, pulling him from his thoughts. He turned to see a figure emerging from the shadows, robes flowing as they moved with purpose. It was Caiaphas, the high priest, flanked by two others whose faces were obscured by their hoods.

Judas's pulse quickened. "What is this about?" he asked, his tone wary.

Caiaphas offered a placating smile, but there was an edge to his expression. "We've been watching you, Judas. You're a man of practical mind, are you not?"

Judas narrowed his eyes. "I'm a man who wants what's best for our people. What do you want with me?"

The high priest gestured toward the stone bench at the edge of the courtyard. "Please, sit. We only wish to speak."

Reluctantly, Judas complied, though he kept a careful distance. Caiaphas sat across from him, folding his hands in his lap. The two other priests remained standing, their silence adding to the tension.

"You travel with the teacher from Nazareth," Caiaphas began, his tone conversational. "Jesus, they call him. He's grown quite popular, hasn't he?"

Judas nodded cautiously. "He has. His words give people hope."

Caiaphas's smile tightened. "Hope can be dangerous in the wrong hands."

Judas's brow furrowed. "What are you saying?"

The high priest leaned forward, his voice lowering. "You've seen the crowds. You've heard their whispers. They call him a king, Judas. A messiah. Do you know what that means? Do you know what Rome will do if they believe a revolt is brewing?"

Judas's stomach twisted. He'd thought of this before, late at night when his doubts gnawed at him. "Jesus isn't leading a revolt. He preaches peace."

Caiaphas's eyes gleamed. "Do you think Rome cares what he preaches? They will see the crowds, the adoration, and they will act. When they do, it won't just be him they destroy. They will come for all of us. Our temple. Our people. Our children."

The words hit Judas like a blow. He swallowed hard, his throat dry. "What are you asking me to do?"

"We are not asking for much," Caiaphas said smoothly. "Only information. Help us understand where he will be, when he is vulnerable. If we act swiftly, we can contain this before it spirals out of control."

Judas shook his head, his voice rising. "You want me to betray him."

Caiaphas raised his hand, his expression calm. "No, Judas. We want you to save our people. One man's sacrifice could save thousands."

Judas's chest tightened, his mind racing. "And who decides whose life is worth more? Yours? Mine?"

The high priest's gaze didn't waver. "Sometimes, the burden of such decisions falls on those strong enough to bear it."

Judas stood abruptly; his fists clenched. "You think this is strength? Manipulation? Deception? That's not strength. That's cowardice."

Caiaphas rose slowly, his expression softening, though his voice remained firm. "You misunderstand. This is not about us. It is about what is at stake. If you care for your people, Judas, you will consider what I have said. The alternative is far worse."

Judas stared at him, his breathing heavy. For a moment, he wanted to walk away, to leave this conversation behind and pretend it had never happened. But the words lingered, their weight pressing down on him.

Finally, he spoke, his voice barely above a whisper. "I'll think about it."

Caiaphas nodded, his smile returning. "That is all we ask."

CHAPTER 12: THE BETRAYAL

The temple courtyard was quiet, bathed in the soft glow of moonlight. Judas lingered at the gates, his heart pounding as he debated whether to step inside. The weight of his thoughts felt heavier than ever, the words of Jesus from the last supper still echoing in his mind.

Finally, he squared his shoulders and entered, his footsteps echoing off the stone walls. The air inside was cold, the vast emptiness of the temple amplifying the unease in his chest. He was greeted by a servant who quickly led him to an inner chamber, where several priests were gathered.

Caiaphas stood at the center, his expression calm but sharp, as if he had been expecting Judas.

"Judas," Caiaphas said, his voice smooth. "What brings you here at this hour?"

Judas hesitated, his gaze darting around the room. He swallowed hard before speaking. "You... you said Jesus is dangerous. That his teachings could bring ruin to our people."

Caiaphas nodded slowly, his gaze unwavering. "Indeed. His growing influence stirs unrest, Judas. Rome watches closely, waiting for any sign of rebellion. If they perceive him as a threat, they will act without mercy."

"He's not a threat," Judas replied, though his voice wavered. "He speaks of peace, not war."

One of the priests, an older man with a gruff demeanor, stepped forward. "And yet, the crowds grow larger with each passing day. They call him the Messiah, a king. Do you not see what this means? Rome will not distinguish between words of peace and words of rebellion."

Judas looked away, his mind racing. The priests exchanged glances before Caiaphas spoke again.

"Judas, you know him well. You've walked beside him. Surely, you see the danger he poses—not just to himself, but to all of us. To our people."

"What are you asking of me?" Judas asked, his voice barely above a whisper.

Caiaphas stepped closer; his tone soft but insistent. "Help us. Tell us where we can find him, when he is vulnerable. If we act swiftly, we can prevent greater harm. This is not betrayal, Judas. It is a necessary step to protect what we hold dear."

Judas's chest tightened. "And what will happen to him?"

The priests exchanged another glance before Caiaphas replied. "That is for the council to decide. He will be questioned, given a chance to explain himself. But his path cannot continue as it is."

Judas's hands trembled. He wanted to believe them, to trust that this was the right course of action. But a voice deep within him screamed in protest.

"We do not ask this lightly," Caiaphas continued, his voice tinged with urgency. "You have the power to prevent disaster, Judas. To save countless lives."

Another priest stepped forward, holding a small pouch. The soft clink of coins was unmistakable as he placed it in Judas's hand. "Consider this an offering of gratitude."

Judas stared at the pouch, the silver gleaming faintly in the dim light. His breath quickened as he clenched it tightly.

"I... I'll do it," he stammered, stepping back toward the door.

Caiaphas nodded; his expression unreadable. "Do what you must, Judas. But remember, time is of the essence."

Judas left the chamber, the weight of the silver and the priests' words pressing heavily on him. As he walked through the dark streets of Jerusalem, his mind churned with doubt and guilt. He told himself it wasn't betrayal. It was duty. It was protection. It was… salvation.

But no matter how many times he repeated the words, they felt hollow, their weight threatening to crush him entirely.

CHAPTER 13: THE LAST SUPPER

The room was warm, lit by the flickering glow of oil lamps and the low hum of conversation among the disciples. The scent of roasted lamb and fresh bread filled the air, mingling with the faint tang of wine. Judas sat at the far end of the long table, his gaze fixed on the cup in his hands. His fingers traced its rim absently as the voices of the others seemed to fade into the background.

Jesus sat at the center, his calm presence grounding the room despite the undercurrent of tension. He had spoken earlier of suffering, of betrayal, words that had cast a shadow over what was meant to be a celebration of Passover.

Judas's chest tightened as he watched Jesus break the bread, his movements deliberate, almost reverent. He wanted to look away but found himself unable to. The weight of his secret felt suffocating, pressing against his ribs with every breath.

"Take and eat," Jesus said, his voice steady but tinged with sorrow. He held the bread out, his gaze sweeping over the group. "This is my body, given for you. Do this in remembrance of me."

The disciples accepted the bread in silence, their expressions ranging from reverence to confusion. Judas hesitated, his hand hovering over the piece offered to him. When Jesus's eyes met his, a jolt ran through him. It was as if Jesus could see every corner of his soul, every dark thought he had tried to bury.

"Take it, Judas," Jesus said softly.

Judas's hand trembled as he took the bread, his throat dry. He placed it in his mouth, chewing mechanically, the taste turning to ash on his tongue.

Later, as the meal continued, Jesus lifted the cup of wine, his expression solemn. "This cup is the new covenant in my blood, poured out for many for the forgiveness of sins. Drink from it, all of you."

Judas watched as the cup was passed around, each disciple drinking deeply. When it reached him, he stared at the dark liquid, its surface shimmering in the lamplight. He hesitated, the weight of Jesus's earlier words ringing in his ears.

"One of you will betray me," Jesus had said. The room had fallen silent, the disciples looking at one another in shock.

"Lord, is it I?" Peter had asked, his voice tight with disbelief.

"The one who has dipped his hand into the bowl with me will betray me," Jesus had replied, his tone heavy with sorrow

The words echoed in Judas's mind as he lifted the cup to his lips. The wine burned as he swallowed, its taste sharp and bitter.

The meal continued, but the atmosphere was strained. Jesus spoke of love and service, of the need to be a servant to others. He knelt to wash their feet, an act that left them humbled and confused.

When he came to Judas, their eyes met again. Judas's breath hitched as Jesus knelt before him, the basin of water in his hands.

"You don't have to do this," Judas said, his voice barely audible.

"Yes, I do," Jesus replied, his tone unwavering.

As the water washed over his feet, Judas felt a wave of shame so intense it left him trembling. He wanted to speak, to confess, to beg for forgiveness, but the words lodged in his throat.

When the meal ended, Jesus rose, his expression resolute. "The time has come. Let us go."

The disciples followed him out into the night, their footsteps echoing in the narrow streets. Judas lingered at the back, his heart pounding. Each step felt like a march toward his own destruction.

As they approached the garden of Gethsemane, Judas slowed, his mind racing. He knew what he had to do. The pieces were already in motion, and there was no turning back. But as he watched Jesus walk ahead, his figure illuminated by the pale light of the moon, Judas felt a pang of doubt that threatened to undo him.

"Forgive me," he whispered to the night, though he wasn't sure if he was asking Jesus, God, or himself.

The garden loomed ahead, its shadows deep and foreboding. Judas took a deep breath, steeling himself. The time was near, and his role in it could no longer be denied.

CHAPTER 14: THE GARDEN CONFRONTATION

The garden was quiet, the only sounds were the rustle of leaves and the faint chirping of crickets. The disciples were scattered throughout, some resting, others keeping watch. Judas moved silently among them, his steps deliberate, his mind a storm of thoughts. The weight of the silver coins in his pocket felt heavier with each step.

He found Jesus kneeling beneath an ancient olive tree, his face turned upward as if seeking the heavens. The moonlight filtered through the branches, casting soft shadows across his serene features. For a moment, Judas hesitated, caught between the urge to speak and the fear of what might follow.

"Jesus," he called softly.

Jesus turned; his eyes calm but weary. "Judas. Come sit with me."

Judas approached, his heart pounding. He lowered himself to the ground, the rough bark of the tree pressing against his back as he leaned against it. For a moment, neither of them spoke, the silence stretching between them like a taut thread.

Finally, Judas broke the quiet. "Do you not care what happens to us?"

Jesus's gaze remained steady. "I care more than you will ever know."

The words stung, their sincerity cutting through Judas's

frustration. "Then why do you continue down this path? You see the danger. The priests, Rome—they're watching you. Waiting for a reason to act. If you keep going, they will destroy you. And us."

Jesus turned his eyes toward the sky, his expression thoughtful. "Do you believe destruction is the end, Judas?"

"It's the end of everything we've built," Judas replied sharply. "The crowds, the hope you've given them... it will all turn to ashes. Is that what you want?"

Jesus's voice softened. "Hope is not a flame that can be extinguished by the winds of this world. It is a light that endures, even in the darkest places."

Judas's fists clenched at his sides. "You speak in riddles. Always riddles. Do you not see how much they need you? How much we need you? If you fall, who will lead us?"

Jesus turned to him; his eyes filled with a quiet intensity. "It is not I who will lead, but the truth. And the truth will endure, even if I do not."

The words struck Judas like a blow. He leaned forward, his voice rising with desperation. "But why? Why must it be this way? Why not fight? Why not show them your power, make them see what you can do? You could stop this. You could save us all."

Jesus reached out, placing a hand on Judas's shoulder. His touch was firm, steady. "Saving you does not mean sparing you from suffering, Judas. It means guiding you through it. Showing you that there is more beyond it."

Tears pricked at the corners of Judas's eyes, though he refused to let them fall. "And what of us? What of those who believe in you, who have left everything to follow you? Will you abandon us to save your kingdom?"

"I am not abandoning you," Jesus said gently. "But the path ahead is not one I can walk for you. Each of you must choose it for yourselves."

Judas pulled away, shaking his head. "You're asking too much. You're asking us to give everything, to risk everything, for what? A promise of something we can't even, see?"

Jesus's expression didn't waver. "Faith, Judas. Faith in what cannot yet be seen. In what cannot yet be understood."

Judas stood abruptly, his chest heaving. "I don't know if I can do that. I don't know if I can follow you into the dark, not knowing where it will lead."

Jesus rose slowly, his movements deliberate. He stepped closer, his gaze piercing but kind. "You are not alone, Judas. The light you seek is within you. Even in the darkest places, it will guide you, if you let it."

For a moment, Judas was silent, his mind a whirlwind of doubt and fear. Finally, he shook his head, his voice trembling. "I can't. I can't follow a path that leads only to death."

Jesus's hand fell to his side. He nodded, his expression calm but tinged with sorrow. "Then do what you must."

The words struck Judas like a blow, the finality of them cutting through his confusion. He turned and walked away, his steps heavy, his heart torn. Behind him, Jesus remained beneath the olive tree, his figure bathed in moonlight.

Judas wandered the garden, his mind a storm of emotions. The weight of the silver coins pressed against his side, a reminder of the choice that loomed before him. He told himself it wasn't betrayal. It was practicality. It was a necessity. It was… sacrifice.

But no matter how many times he repeated the words, they felt hollow, their comfort fleeting. Deep down, a quiet voice whispered something else. Something he couldn't bear to hear.

CHAPTER 15: THE FATEFUL KISS

The garden was still, save for the faint rustle of olive leaves in the cool night breeze. The disciples rested uneasily, their voices and movements subdued after the weight of Jesus's earlier words. Judas approached the garden's edge, his steps hesitant and his heart heavy. Behind him, the clink of armor and the soft murmur of soldiers' voices served as an ominous reminder of the decision he had made.

The temple guards, led by a stern-faced officer, waited in the shadows. Caiaphas's silver weighed heavily in Judas's pocket, each coin feeling like a stone dragging him deeper into despair. As they reached the outskirts of the garden, the officer turned to him.

"You know what to do," the officer said curtly.

Judas nodded; his throat too tight to speak. His hands trembled as he turned back toward the olive grove, the silhouettes of the disciples visible in the moonlight. His eyes sought out Jesus, who knelt beneath a familiar tree, his figure bathed in a serene glow. The sight made Judas's chest tighten, but he forced himself to move forward.

Jesus's head lifted as Judas approached, his expression calm despite the tension that hung in the air. The disciples stirred, their murmurs rising in confusion as they noticed the figures emerging from the shadows.

"Judas," Peter called, his voice low but urgent. "What's going on?"

Judas didn't answer. His gaze remained fixed on Jesus, who rose slowly, his movements deliberate. The other disciples stepped forward protectively, but Jesus raised a hand, stopping them in their tracks.

"Friend," Jesus said, his voice steady, "why have you come?"

The word cut through Judas like a blade. He swallowed hard, his lips trembling as he tried to form a response. Instead, he stepped closer, the distance between them shrinking until he stood just a breath away.

"Forgive me," Judas whispered, his voice breaking.

Before Jesus could respond, Judas leaned in, pressing a kiss to his cheek. The act was simple, fleeting, but its weight was crushing. Jesus's eyes met his, and in them, Judas saw not anger or betrayal, but sorrow and understanding.

The soldiers surged forward, their movements swift and practiced. They grabbed Jesus, binding his hands as the disciples erupted in protest.

"What are you doing?" Peter shouted, drawing a sword and stepping toward the guards. He slashed at one of them, the blade cutting through the man's ear.

"Enough!" Jesus commanded, his voice firm. He turned to Peter, his gaze stern but compassionate. "Put your sword back in its place. Those who live by the sword will die by the sword."

Peter froze, his chest heaving, as Jesus bent down beside the injured soldier. With a calmness that seemed almost otherworldly, Jesus reached out, his hand hovering over the bleeding wound. The soldier flinched but did not move as Jesus's touch brought a warmth that spread across the injury.

When Jesus withdrew his hand, the ear was whole again, the blood gone as if it had never been. The soldier stared at him in stunned silence, his hand tentatively reaching up to feel the healed flesh.

"Who are you?" the soldier whispered, his voice trembling.

Jesus rose, his expression serene. "I am the one you seek. Let these others go."

The soldiers hesitated, their gazes flicking between Jesus and their leader. Finally, the officer nodded, and they moved to bind Jesus's hands. The disciples watched in horrified silence; their protests stifled by Jesus's steady gaze.

Judas stepped back, his legs trembling. The sight of Jesus healing the very man who had come to arrest him only deepened the chasm of guilt within him. He turned away, unable to watch as they led Jesus away into the night.

As the soldiers led Jesus away, Judas lingered in the garden, the weight of his actions pressing down on him. The disciples' accusatory glares burned into his back, but he couldn't bring himself to face them. Instead, he sank to his knees beneath the olive tree, the same spot where he had confronted Jesus just hours before.

"What have I done?" he whispered, his voice barely audible. The words echoed in his mind, each repetition hammering home the gravity of his betrayal.

The memory of Jesus's eyes haunted him. He had expected anger, condemnation, perhaps even hatred. But instead, he had seen only sadness and... love. The realization twisted the knife in Judas's heart, leaving him gasping for air.

The disciples gathered nearby; their voices hushed but frantic.

"Why did he do it?" John asked, his voice trembling. "Why would Judas betray him?"

Peter's face was dark with anger. "He was always questioning, always doubting. Maybe he never truly believed."

"Enough," Andrew said, his tone sharp. "This isn't the time to turn on each other. We need to figure out what to do next."

Judas heard their words but couldn't bring himself to respond. He pressed his forehead to the ground, his tears soaking into the earth. The silver coins spilled from his pocket, clinking softly as they scattered across the dirt.

As the night deepened, Judas rose unsteadily to his feet. He stared at the coins, their gleam mocking him in the moonlight. His mind churned with regret, self-loathing, and the unbearable weight of what he had set into motion.

"Forgive me," he murmured again, though he knew the words would not undo what had been done. He turned and walked away from the garden, his steps heavy, his heart shattered.

The night was quiet once more, but for Judas, there would be no peace.

CHAPTER 16: CONDEMNED BY HISTORY

The temple courtyard was quiet except for the faint flicker of torches along the stone walls. Judas stormed through the gates, his footsteps echoing with the weight of his fury. In his hand, the bag of silver coins swung violently, the sound of metal clinking against itself a constant reminder of his shame.

Caiaphas and several other priests stood near the altar, their robes pristine and faces composed, as if they had not just orchestrated the arrest of an innocent man. Judas approached them, his face flushed with anger and despair.

"Judas," Caiaphas greeted him, his voice smooth. "You return so soon."

Judas didn't bother with formalities. He threw the bag of silver at their feet, the coins scattering across the marble floor with a deafening clatter. "Take it back!" he shouted. "I want no part of this."

The priests exchanged glances; their expressions unreadable. Caiaphas stepped forward; his hands clasped in front of him. "What troubles you, Judas?"

"You promised salvation," Judas spat, his voice trembling with rage. "But all you've brought is death. You said this would save our people, but you've condemned an innocent man."

Caiaphas's expression remained calm. "The decision was yours,

Judas. We did not force your hand."

Judas's fists clenched. "You manipulated me! You spoke of duty, of sacrifice, of saving lives. But this—this is nothing but murder."

"It is justice," another priest interjected, his tone cold. "This man —this Jesus—threatened the stability of our people. His growing influence would have brought Rome's wrath upon us all."

Judas shook his head, his voice breaking. "You don't understand. He wasn't leading a rebellion. He was trying to save us in ways you'll never comprehend."

Caiaphas stepped closer, his eyes narrowing. "And yet you delivered him to us. You knew the consequences, Judas. Do not feign innocence now."

"I didn't know it would feel like this," Judas whispered, his voice barely audible. He stared at the scattered coins, their gleam mocking him under the torchlight. "I thought I was doing what was right… for the people, for him. But I was wrong."

"Your choices are your own," Caiaphas said, his voice dismissive. "We cannot undo what has been done. The matter is out of your hands."

Judas's eyes burned with tears as he looked at the priests, their faces devoid of remorse. "You call this justice? You're cowards. Hiding behind Rome, behind laws you twist to suit your purpose. You've killed him… and for what? To protect your positions? Your power?"

Caiaphas's expression darkened. "Enough, Judas. Leave, before you bring more shame upon yourself."

Judas stared at them, his chest heaving with the weight of his guilt and anger. Then, without another word, he turned and fled, his footsteps echoing through the empty courtyard.

The streets of Jerusalem were silent, the city asleep under the blanket of night. Judas wandered aimlessly, his mind a storm of emotions. The image of Jesus's calm, sorrowful eyes as he was led away replayed endlessly in his mind, each iteration cutting deeper than the last.

He found himself at the edge of the city, overlooking the valley below. The cool night air did little to soothe the fire raging within him. He sank to the ground, his head in his hands, the weight of his actions pressing down on him like a crushing burden.

"What have I done?" he whispered to the night. His voice broke, the words lost in the vast emptiness around him. He thought of the disciples, of their trust in him. He thought of Jesus, who had called him "friend" even as he delivered him to his enemies.

The coins he had thrown at the priests' feet felt as if they still clung to him, their weight dragging him deeper into despair. He couldn't escape them, couldn't escape himself.

As dawn approached, Judas rose unsteadily to his feet. The first rays of light painted the horizon in shades of gold and pink, a cruel reminder of a new day. He walked back toward the city, his steps heavy, his heart hollow.

The streets began to stir with life, merchants setting up their stalls, children running through the alleys. Judas avoided their eyes, his shame a constant shadow at his back. He didn't know where he was going, only that he couldn't stay still. He needed to escape the torment within him, though he knew it would follow wherever he went.

As he passed the temple gates, the sounds of morning prayers drifted through the air. Judas paused, his gaze drawn to the holy place that now felt so far removed from anything sacred. He clenched his fists, his nails digging into his palms as a fresh wave of anguish washed over him.

"Forgive me," he murmured, though he didn't know who he was asking—God, Jesus, or himself. The words felt empty, their weight unable to match the depth of his guilt.

He turned and walked away, the sound of the city fading as he disappeared into the distance. Judas didn't look back.

CHAPTER 17: HAUNTED BY GHOSTS

The small room was dark and silent, save for the faint creak of the wooden floorboards beneath Judas's restless pacing. His steps were uneven, his breaths shallow and erratic. Outside, the night pressed heavily against the windows, its stillness a stark contrast to the storm raging within him.

He hadn't slept since that night in the garden. Every time he closed his eyes, he saw Jesus's face, calm and sorrowful, staring at him as if piercing through to the depths of his soul. The memory of the soldiers binding Jesus's hands replayed in his mind, each iteration more vivid, more unbearable.

"Was it me, or was it fate?" Judas whispered to the empty room, his voice trembling. His question hung in the air, unanswered, taunting him.

He stopped pacing and sank into a chair by the window, his head in his hands. The weight of his actions pressed down on him like an unbearable burden. The faces of the disciples floated in his mind, their expressions a mixture of shock and betrayal. He could almost hear Peter's voice, sharp and accusing: *You were always questioning, always doubting.*

Judas slammed his fist against the table, the sudden noise shattering the silence. "No!" he shouted, his voice hoarse. "I didn't mean for this! I didn't..." His voice broke, the words dissolving into a choked sob.

The room seemed to close in around him, the shadows growing

darker, deeper. He glanced toward the corner, where he thought he saw a figure standing. His breath caught, his heart pounding in his chest.

"Who's there?" he demanded, his voice shaking.

The figure didn't move, but as Judas stared, it began to take shape. It was Jesus, his face pale and serene, his eyes filled with the same sorrowful understanding that had haunted Judas since the garden.

"Why?" the vision of Jesus asked, his voice soft but steady. "Why did you do it, Judas?"

Judas backed away, his hands trembling. "I didn't want to," he stammered. "I thought... I thought it was the right thing. I thought it would save us."

"Did you?" the figure asked, stepping closer. "Or were you trying to save yourself?"

The words cut through Judas like a blade. He shook his head, tears streaming down his face. "No! I wanted to protect you, to protect everyone. They said it was the only way."

"And now?" the vision said, its tone unchanged. "Do you see the truth?"

Judas fell to his knees, his body wracked with sobs. "I see it," he whispered. "But it's too late. I can't take it back."

The vision of Jesus knelt before him, reaching out to place a hand on Judas's shoulder. The touch felt real, warm, and Judas looked up, his tear-filled eyes meeting the figure's gaze.

"It is never too late to seek forgiveness," the vision said. "But forgiveness must start within."

The words echoed in Judas's mind as the figure faded, leaving him alone once more. The room was silent, save for the sound of his ragged breathing.

Judas rose unsteadily, his legs trembling. He staggered to the door and stepped outside, the cool night air hitting his face like a slap.

He wandered aimlessly through the empty streets of Jerusalem, the city's silence amplifying the noise in his mind.

The voices came then, insidious whispers that seemed to come from nowhere and everywhere at once.

"Betrayer."

"Coward."

"You have blood on your hands."

Judas clutched his head, shaking it violently as if to drive the voices away. "Leave me alone!" he cried, his voice echoing off the stone walls.

The whispers grew louder, overlapping and relentless. Images of Jesus flashed before his eyes: his smile as he taught the crowds, his patience as he answered questions, his sorrow as he accepted Judas's kiss. Each image was a dagger, stabbing deeper into Judas's soul.

He found himself at the edge of the valley, the same spot he had stood after fleeing the temple. The horizon was just beginning to lighten, the first hints of dawn painting the sky in shades of gray and blue. Judas sank to his knees, his body shaking with the force of his sobs.

"Was it me, or was it fate?" he whispered again, his voice breaking. "Did I choose this, or was it chosen for me?"

The wind carried no answer, only the rustle of leaves and the distant call of a bird. Judas closed his eyes, the weight of his guilt pressing down on him like a crushing tide. The vision's words echoed in his mind: *It is never too late to seek forgiveness.*

But Judas didn't know if he could forgive himself. And without that, he wondered, could anyone else?

The first rays of sunlight broke over the horizon, casting long shadows across the valley. Judas remained on his knees, his heart heavy, his soul fractured. The day had begun, but for Judas, there would be no light.

CHAPTER 18: THE JOURNEY FOR REDEMPTION

The morning air was cold as Judas left Jerusalem behind; his steps heavy on the dusty road. He carried nothing but a staff, a small flask of water, and the unbearable weight of his guilt. Each step felt like penance, a painful reminder of the man he had been and the choices that had brought him to this moment.

His destination was unclear. Perhaps he sought forgiveness. Perhaps he sought punishment. He only knew that staying in the city, surrounded by the echoes of his betrayal, was impossible.

The first encounter came as he neared a bend in the road, where the figure of a man lay crumpled on the ground. Judas approached cautiously, his hand tightening on his staff. The man was clad in the armor of a Roman soldier, his leg twisted at an unnatural angle, blood seeping from a gash on his forehead.

"Help me," the soldier rasped, his voice weak.

Judas hesitated, his heart pounding. A part of him screamed to leave, to let the man suffer as so many of his own people had suffered at the hands of Rome. But another part—a quieter, insistent voice—urged him to stay.

Kneeling beside the soldier, Judas tore a strip of cloth from his tunic and pressed it to the wound. The soldier winced, his hand gripping Judas's arm.

"Why… why are you helping me?" the soldier asked, his tone suspicious.

Judas didn't look up. "Because you're injured. That's reason enough."

The soldier's grip loosened, and he fell silent, watching as Judas worked. When the wound was bound and the soldier's leg splinted as best as Judas could manage, he rose to his feet.

"There's a village not far from here," Judas said. "If you're strong enough, you'll find help there."

The soldier nodded weakly. "Thank you."

Judas didn't respond. He turned and continued down the road, the soldier's faint gratitude trailing after him like a whisper.

Days later, Judas found himself in a small village nestled in the hills. The air was thick with the scent of wood smoke and freshly tilled earth. He stopped at the edge of the village, his gaze drawn to a woman sitting on the ground, her face buried in her hands. A small wooden cart, its contents spilled across the dirt, lay overturned beside her.

Judas approached cautiously. "Are you hurt?" he asked.

The woman looked up, her eyes red-rimmed and filled with grief. "No," she said, her voice trembling. "But my son… he's gone. Taken by fever. I was bringing his things to the healer to bless them, but…" She gestured helplessly at the cart.

Judas felt a pang in his chest. He crouched beside her, lifting the overturned cart and carefully gathering the scattered items. The woman watched him, her expression wary.

"Why are you helping me?" she asked.

Judas hesitated, the question striking a nerve. "Because I can," he said finally.

When the cart was righted, he stood and looked at the woman, his heart heavy. "I'm sorry for your loss," he said.

She nodded, her lips pressing into a thin line. "Thank you." As she turned to leave, she paused and looked back at him. "Forgiveness isn't earned," she said softly. "It's given."

The words struck Judas like a blow, but before he could respond, the woman walked away, her cart creaking as it rolled down the path.

That night, Judas sat by a small fire, the woman's words echoing in his mind. "Forgiveness isn't earned; it's given." Could it be true? Could he, a man who had betrayed the one person who had believed in him, ever be forgiven?

His thoughts were interrupted by the sound of footsteps. A ragged figure emerged from the shadows—a beggar, his clothes tattered and his face gaunt.

"Spare some food?" the beggar asked, his voice thin.

Judas hesitated, then reached into his bag and handed the man a piece of bread. The beggar took it eagerly, devouring it with trembling hands. When he was finished, he looked at Judas with a faint smile.

"Thank you," he said. "You have a kind heart."

Judas looked away, the words cutting deep. "You don't know me."

The beggar chuckled softly. "Maybe not. But kindness is rare these days. It speaks louder than anything else."

As the beggar disappeared into the night, Judas stared into the flames, his mind churning. Each encounter had chipped away at the walls he had built around his heart, forcing him to confront the man he had become.

By the time the sun rose, Judas felt a small, fragile seed of hope stirring within him. His journey was far from over, but for the first time, he wondered if forgiveness—for himself and from others—might not be as unattainable as he had believed.

CHAPTER 19: A VISION OF TRUTH

The world around Judas was cloaked in shadows, a surreal blend of reality and dream. He walked a path that seemed endless, the horizon shifting with each step. The air was heavy, not with heat or cold, but with a weight that pressed against his chest, making it hard to breathe.

Then he saw Him.

Jesus stood in the distance, his figure illuminated by a light that seemed to come from nowhere and everywhere. His face was calm, serene, as it had been in life. Judas's heart pounded in his chest as he moved closer, his steps faltering. He wasn't sure if this was real or a product of his tormented mind, but he couldn't stop himself.

When he was close enough to see the lines of Jesus's face, the sorrow in his eyes, Judas dropped to his knees.

"Why?" Judas's voice cracked, the word escaping in a whisper. "Why did you let me do it? Why didn't you stop me?"

Jesus looked at him, his gaze piercing but gentle. "Would you have listened if I had?"

Judas's hands clenched into fists. "I don't know! I thought... I thought I was doing the right thing. They told me it was the only way to save you, to save us all."

Jesus knelt before him, the light surrounding him softening as he reached out a hand to Judas's shoulder. The touch was warm, grounding.

"You carried the weight I gave you, Judas," Jesus said, his voice steady. "But the burden was always mine."

Judas looked up, his eyes brimming with tears. "What does that mean? Was it fate? Was it my choice? Tell me, was I doomed to betray you from the start?"

Jesus's expression didn't waver. "You were given a path, just as we all are. But the steps you took were yours alone."

The words struck Judas like a blow. He recoiled, shaking his head. "Then I chose this? I chose to betray you? To deliver you to them?"

"Yes," Jesus said softly. "And no. Your choices were shaped by the weight you bore, the questions you carried. But the path was never without purpose."

Judas's chest heaved as he struggled to breathe through his anguish. "Purpose?" he spat. "What purpose could there be in betrayal?"

"The purpose of love," Jesus replied. "To show the world that even in its darkest hour, forgiveness can shine through."

Judas's hands trembled as he covered his face. "I don't deserve forgiveness. Not from you, not from anyone. I betrayed you. I destroyed everything."

Jesus reached out, gently pulling Judas's hands away from his face. "Forgiveness is not about deserving, Judas. It is about giving. And I give it freely to you."

Judas shook his head, tears streaming down his cheeks. "I can't forgive myself."

Jesus's gaze softened further. "Then let my forgiveness be enough. Let it begin where you cannot."

The air grew heavier, the light around them intensifying. Judas felt as though the ground beneath him were dissolving, the surreal world tilting on its axis. He clung to Jesus's words, to the warmth of his presence, even as it began to fade.

When Judas opened his eyes, he was lying on the ground, the first rays of dawn breaking over the horizon. The world was quiet, the surreal vision replaced by the tangible weight of morning.

He sat up slowly, his body aching as though he had walked for miles. The words Jesus had spoken lingered in his mind, a soft echo that refused to fade.

"You carried the weight I gave you, but the burden was always mine."

For the first time in days, Judas felt a strange, tentative sense of peace. The questions still lingered, the guilt still gnawed at him, but there was something else now. A small, fragile spark of hope.

He rose to his feet, brushing the dirt from his clothes. His journey wasn't over, but perhaps, he thought, it was only just beginning.

CHAPTER 20: THE FINAL DECISION

The morning light spilled across the hills as Judas sat alone, his back pressed against a weathered olive tree. The vision of Jesus lingered in his mind, vivid and unrelenting, as if etched into his very soul. He had spent the night wrestling with its meaning, the words repeating over and over like a haunting refrain.

You carried the weight I gave you, but the burden was always mine.

Judas looked down at his hands, calloused and trembling. They had been tools of betrayal, instruments of his own downfall. He clenched them into fists, as if trying to trap the guilt that threatened to consume him.

"If even He could forgive me," Judas murmured, his voice barely audible, "why can't I?"

The path before him was steep and rocky, winding its way toward a ridge overlooking the valley. Judas had no clear destination, but his feet carried him forward as if driven by some unseen force. He passed a shepherd tending his flock, who nodded a quiet greeting. The simple kindness stung more than any accusation.

As Judas climbed higher, his thoughts swirled in a storm of doubt and self-recrimination. The faces of those he had betrayed—Jesus, the disciples, even himself—floated before him, their expressions a blend of sorrow and condemnation.

"What do you want from me?" he cried out to the empty sky. His voice echoed, swallowed by the vastness of the landscape. "What more can I give?"

The wind answered with a soft, mournful whisper, carrying the scent of wildflowers and earth. Judas sank to his knees, his strength failing him. He buried his face in his hands, the tears coming freely now.

He didn't hear the old man approach until he spoke.

"You look like a man with a heavy heart," the stranger said, his voice rough but kind.

Judas looked up, startled. The man was hunched with age, his face lined with wrinkles that spoke of a life hard-lived. He carried a walking stick, its surface smooth from years of use.

"Who are you?" Judas asked, his voice hoarse.

"A traveler," the man replied, settling onto a rock nearby. "Like you, I suspect. Though it seems your journey is a heavier one."

Judas said nothing, his gaze returning to the ground. The old man studied him for a moment, then spoke again.

"Sometimes, the hardest journey isn't the one we walk with our feet," he said. "It's the one we walk in here." He tapped his chest with a gnarled finger.

Judas let out a bitter laugh. "And what if that journey has no end? What if the weight is too much to bear?"

The old man leaned forward, his eyes sharp despite their age. "Then you lay it down. Not because you deserve to, but because carrying it forever serves no one—least of all yourself."

Judas's throat tightened. "I don't know how."

The man smiled faintly. "Start by forgiving the man who brought you here."

The ridge overlooked a sprawling valley, its lush greenery a stark contrast to the barren terrain Judas had traversed. He stood at the edge, the wind tugging at his tunic, and gazed down at the world below. It seemed vast, eternal, indifferent to the turmoil within him.

He thought of Jesus—his teachings, his kindness, his sacrifice. He thought of the disciples, their trust in him shattered by his betrayal. And he thought of himself, a man torn between the weight of his guilt and the faint glimmer of hope that forgiveness might be possible.

Judas took a deep breath, the air filling his lungs like a balm. He closed his eyes and whispered the words that had eluded him for so long.

"I forgive you."

The wind carried the words away, scattering them across the valley like seeds. Judas didn't know if they would take root, if they would grow into something that could heal the wounds he had inflicted. But for the first time, he felt a sliver of light pierce the darkness within him.

The path down from the ridge was slow and deliberate. Each step felt like a choice, a decision to move forward despite the weight he still carried. The burden wasn't gone, but it felt lighter, as if shared by something greater than himself.

As Judas reached the base of the hill, the sun broke fully over the horizon, bathing the world in golden light. He paused, turning his face toward the warmth, and let it wash over him.

His journey wasn't over. The questions remained; the pain lingered. But for the first time, Judas felt that perhaps he could find his way—not to absolution, but to acceptance. And in that, he found a fragile, tenuous peace.

AFTERWORD

The Lost Disciple is not just a story of Judas Iscariot; it is a story about all of us. It delves into the complexities of human emotion, the struggle between faith and doubt, and the consequences of choices made under the weight of fear and ambition. Judas's story reminds us that history often defines individuals by a single act, but humanity is far more complex than any one moment.

In exploring Judas's journey, I hoped to challenge the conventional narrative and offer a new perspective—one that sees him as deeply human, not just a symbol of betrayal. His story is a lens through which we can examine our own struggles with morality, forgiveness, and redemption.

I leave it to you, the reader, to decide what to make of Judas. Was he a victim of fate, a pawn in a divine plan, or simply a man who made a grave mistake? Perhaps he was all of these at once.

Thank you for walking this journey with me. I hope this story lingers in your heart, not as a condemnation of one man, but as an invitation to reflect on the complexities of faith, love, and the human condition.

ACKNOWLEDGEMENT

This book has been a journey of discovery, reflection, and collaboration, and it would not have been possible without the support of many remarkable individuals.

To my wife, Subhashini, your unwavering belief in me has been my anchor. Your patience, love, and encouragement have fueled every word on these pages. To my daughter, Sasha, your joy and innocence remind me daily of the beauty in storytelling and the power of hope.

To my friends and family, thank you for being my sounding boards and cheerleaders. Your insights, questions, and faith in this project kept me moving forward even when the path seemed unclear.

A heartfelt thank you to my editor, whose keen eye and thoughtful feedback helped shape this story into what it has become. Your dedication to bringing depth and nuance to these pages is immeasurable.

To my readers, thank you for taking this journey into the heart of *The Lost Disciple*. Your willingness to explore the complexities of Judas's story inspires me to write with honesty and vulnerability.

Finally, to the timeless narrative of history and faith that inspired this novel, I am grateful for the opportunity to reimagine a story that continues to challenge and provoke us. May it spark meaningful conversations and deeper understanding.

ABOUT THE AUTHOR

D. Deckker

Dinesh Deckker is a multifaceted author and educator with a rich academic background and extensive experience in creative writing and education. Holding a BSc Hons in Computer Science, a BA (Hons), and an MBA from prestigious institutions in the UK, Dinesh has dedicated his career to blending technology, education, and literature.

He has further honed his writing skills through a variety of specialized courses. His qualifications include:
• Children Acquiring Literacy Naturally from UC Santa Cruz, USA
• Creative Writing Specialization from Wesleyan University, USA
• Writing for Young Readers Commonwealth Education Trust
• Introduction to Early Childhood from The State University of New York
• Introduction to Psychology from Yale University
• Academic English: Writing Specialization University of California, Irvine,
• Writing and Editing Specialization from University of Michigan
• Writing and Editing: Word Choice University of Michigan
• Sharpened Visions: A Poetry Workshop from CalArts, USA
• Grammar and Punctuation from University of California, Irvine, USA

- Teaching Writing Specialization from Johns Hopkins University
- Advanced Writing from University of California, Irvine, USA
- English for Journalism from University of Pennsylvania, USA
- Creative Writing: The Craft of Character from Wesleyan University, USA
- Creative Writing: The Craft of Setting from Wesleyan University
- Creative Writing: The Craft of Plot from Wesleyan University, USA
- Creative Writing: The Craft of Style from Wesleyan University, USA

Dinesh's diverse educational background and commitment to lifelong learning have equipped him with a deep understanding of various writing styles and educational techniques. His works often reflect his passion for storytelling, education, and technology, making him a versatile and engaging author.

BOOKS BY THIS AUTHOR

Herod: The Architect Of Power

Step into the world of ancient Judea, where power is fleeting, alliances are fragile, and ambition knows no bounds. Herod: The Architect of Power is a masterful work of historical fiction that brings to life one of history's most controversial figures.

Herod the Great is remembered for his monumental achievements—the breathtaking Second Temple, the impregnable fortress of Masada, and the grand port city of Caesarea Maritima. But behind the brilliance lies a man consumed by paranoia, haunted by betrayal, and willing to sacrifice everything to secure his legacy.

The Titan Expedition: A Sci-Fi Adventure Beyond Saturn

n the year 2078, humanity intercepts an enigmatic signal emanating from Titan, Saturn's largest moon. Persistent, intricate, and intelligent, the signal sparks a high-stakes mission to uncover its origin—a journey that could change the course of human history forever.

Led by the determined Captain Elena Vega, the crew of the spacecraft Odyssey embarks on a perilous expedition to Titan. Each member of the team—brilliant scientists, seasoned explorers, and a corporate insider with hidden motives—must confront their own fears, secrets, and ambitions as they venture into the alien depths of space.

The Light Of Bethlehem: A Story Of Hope And Light

Step into the timeless story of Bethlehem with this deeply human retelling of the Nativity. The Light of Bethlehem invites readers to witness the miracle through the eyes of those who were there—Mary, Joseph, the shepherds, and the wise men. This novel beautifully captures their courage, love, and sacrifice, weaving a rich tapestry of hope and resilience.

Mindful Christmas: Practices For A Joyful Holiday

Are you ready to transform your holiday season into a time of peace, connection, and joy? Mindful Christmas is your guide to creating a meaningful and stress-free celebration through the power of mindfulness.

Printed in Great Britain
by Amazon